SEASONS on the FARM

Chelsea Tornetto and Illustrated by Karen Bunting

PUBLISHED by SLEEPING BEAR PRESS™

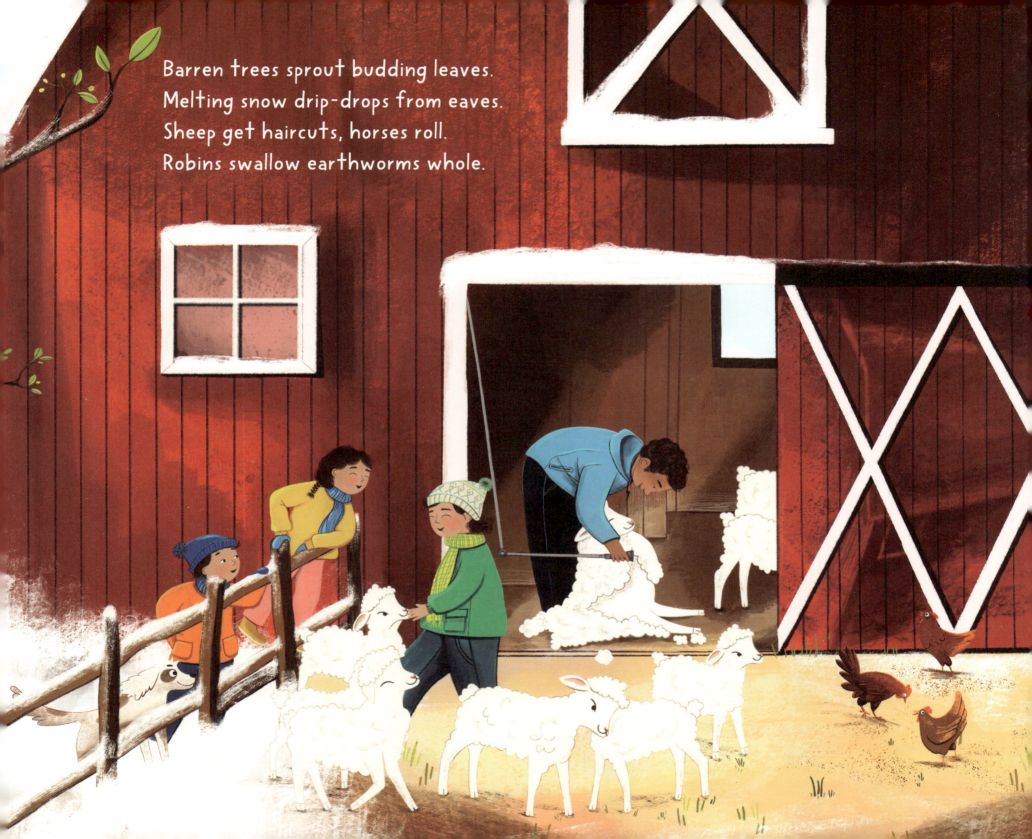

Barren trees sprout budding leaves.
Melting snow drip-drops from eaves.
Sheep get haircuts, horses roll.
Robins swallow earthworms whole.

Muddy fields turn misty green.
Mamas lick their babies clean.

Planting starts when soil is warm.
Signs of springtime on the farm!

Days grow longer, corn grows tall.
Tailgates can do more than haul.

Farmers watch for weeds and rain . . .

Wagons gather golden bales.
Horses swat flies with their tails.

Cornstalks rustle, brown and dry.
Kitchens smell like apple pie.

Combines rumble down long rows;
Into bins the harvest flows.

Leaves are gold and skies are clear.
Pumpkin patches soon appear.

Geese honk winter's first alarm.
Signs of autumn on the farm!

Cold winds blow and skies turn gray.

Tractors stock the lots with hay.

Wood is cut and fires glow.
Fields are covered up with snow.

Gears are oiled and plans are made.
Somehow all the bills get paid.

Mice build nests inside the barn.
Signs of winter on the farm!

Tiny hints and subtle clues,
Things you won't see on the news.

Farmers watch and wait and know
When to harvest, plow, and sow.

Steady as a soaking rain,
Always changing, yet the same.
Part of Mother Nature's charm . . .

Signs of seasons on the farm.

FARMING THROUGH THE SEASONS

Many people in the United States look forward to the changing seasons. Whether it's the beautiful colors of leaves in the fall, the first snowfall of winter, or the appearance of the first daffodil in the spring—each season is fun in its own unique way.

But to farmers, the changing seasons are about much more than fun!

Across America, the arrival of each season brings unique challenges and rewards for farmers and their families. The study of this natural cycle of the seasons and how it impacts animals and plants is called phenology. Part science and part ancient tradition, phenology helps farmers produce successful crops by paying close attention to the changes in temperature, weather, and daylight that come with the changing seasons. After many years or generations of observing this cycle, farmers and their families become expert phenologists! They can recognize and sometimes even predict these signs of the seasons.

SPRING

In spring, farmers begin planting wheat, corn, soybeans, and other grains. The timing of planting is important, because if the soil is too wet or if a frost comes after planting, the seeds may not germinate correctly. Spring is also when many farm animals have babies, sheep are sheared, and fruit trees bloom.

SUMMER

When the days get longer and temperatures get warmer, it's summer on the farm! The main tasks for most farmers during the summer months are monitoring their crops for disease, weeds, and pests and applying pesticides and fertilizers to help keep the plants healthy. Summer can be a season of violent thunderstorms or drought, and some farmers may need to irrigate their fields if it doesn't rain enough. Summer is also when farmers get together to celebrate their successes and compete to see whose crops or animals are the best. State and county fairs are the place to be in the summer!

AUTUMN (FALL)

When the crops have grown to maturity, the weather starts to cool and autumn arrives. Farmers watch carefully and harvest grain when it's dry so it can safely be stored in grain silos for the winter. Grain elevators, where farmers can weigh and sell their crops, are busy this time of year! Other crops, such as apples and pumpkins, are also harvested in the fall, and farmers prepare their animals for the winter months. Sometimes farmers will plant winter wheat, which remains dormant until it sprouts the next spring.

WINTER

Winter might seem like it wouldn't be very busy for farmers since nothing can grow in the cold. But during the winter months, farmers keep busy repairing trucks, tractors, and other equipment and caring for their animals. They make sure that cattle and other livestock have water that's not frozen and hay to eat when the grass is covered with snow. They also use this time to make plans for the next year and research new methods and techniques. Before they know it, the sun begins to shine, the weather gets warmer, and it's springtime—and the cycle of the seasons starts all over again!

For my parents and grandparents—and farm families everywhere.
—Chelsea

For Jack.
—Karen

Text Copyright © 2025 Chelsea Tornetto
Illustration Copyright © 2025 Karen Bunting
Design Copyright © 2025 Sleeping Bear Press

Publisher expressly prohibits the use of this work in connection with the development of any software program, including, without limitation, training a machine learning or generative artificial intelligence (AI) system.

All rights reserved.
No part of this book may be reproduced in any manner without the express written consent of the publisher, except in the case of brief excerpts in critical reviews and articles. All inquiries should be addressed to:

SLEEPING BEAR PRESS™

2395 South Huron Parkway, Suite 200, Ann Arbor, MI 48104
www.sleepingbearpress.com © Sleeping Bear Press

Printed and bound in South Korea
10 9 8 7 6 5 4 3 2 1

Library of Congress Cataloging-in-Publication Data on File
ISBN: 978-1-53411-306-0